THE
Stranger
IN THE LIBRARY
and other Stories

BEVERLEY MEADOWS

The Stranger in the library and other Stories by Beverley Meadows

ISBN 978-1-952027-32-1 (Paperback)
ISBN 978-1-952027-33-8 (Hardback)

This book is written to provide information and motivation to readers. Its purpose is not to render any type of psychological, legal, or professional advice of any kind. The content is the sole opinion and expression of the author, and not necessarily that of the publisher.

Copyright © 2020 by Beverley Meadows

All rights reserved. No part of this book may be reproduced, transmitted, or distributed in any form by any means, including, but not limited to, recording, photocopying, or taking screenshots of parts of the book, without prior written permission from the author or the publisher. Brief quotations for noncommercial purposes, such as book reviews, permitted by Fair Use of the U.S. Copyright Law, are allowed without written permissions, as long as such quotations do not cause damage to the book's commercial value. For permissions, write to the publisher, whose address is stated below.

Printed in the United States of America.

New Leaf Media, LLC
175 S. 3rd Street, Suite 200
Columbus, OH 43215
www.thenewleafmedia.com

Beverley Meadows
21 Showfield
Brampton
Cumbria   CA8 1NY
Tel: (016977 3692)
angelus803@gmail.com

Olympia Publishers
60 Cannon Street
LONDON
EC4N6NP

21st August 2018

Dear Simon

My name is Beverley Meadows, I was born in 1962. When I left school, many years ago, instead of going to university, I accepted a commission in the Royal Air Force. After leaving the Air Force, I took a job in the local doctors' practice as deputy to the Practice Manager, where I stayed for sixteen years. Unfortunately I was diagnosed with MS within my first three years of employment, undeterred I continued at the practice, which I thoroughly enjoyed until it became clear that my illness was getting the better of me.

Like many people, I feel that there is an author within me. I feel uneasy about writing short stories, but let's give it a go!

My writing career, such as it is, is rather limited, but I was one of the winners in the Legend Press 50 word competition in July 2006. I have written various short stories, and have tried self-publication.

My illness is progressive and is therefore getting worse. I am now unable to hold a pen and write legibly; thank goodness for computers and memory sticks!

I sincerely hope that you like my stories and are not deterred, like I sometimes am, by my progressive illness.

Yours sincerely
B A Meadows

The Stranger in the library

By B A Meadows

Is this a story about a remarkable concurrence of events or is it something else? If you read on perhaps it will help you to make up your mind.

Chapter One

I had left university with an English degree and had settled for a short-term job in a library. I actually wanted to travel, but needed to work to save some money. The whole problem is, finding a job that is suitable; the age old question. After what seemed like ages I found work that seemed as if it might be just what I was looking for. I went through all the usual palaver and was eventually offered the position. The job was all right, but it wasn't what I had spent years at university to end up doing. Nevertheless it would do for now.

Everything seemed settled in my world, except that occasionally, I felt that something was missing, I couldn't isolate anything specifically, but I felt incomplete, as if there was something or was it someone that was absent. Perhaps a man was that absent ingredient. Not that I was desperate on that front, but sometimes I wished a tall, handsome stranger would just materialise from nowhere. Delusional or what? I really don't think I am delusional, I think I am just a little sensitive on occasions. I love listening to "Puff the magic dragon" and have listened to it, on and off, for years but it really makes me cry now. It has just dawned on me (better late than never!) that the song is actually about growing up and how your imagination alters as you grow so that what you once believed in you now don't. That poor dragon…

Lucie seemed unsettled, even though her degree had given her some options. Taking the job in the library was meant to be a short-term choice, but it was turning out to be quite a cushy number, and she was happy to stay there. Things were about to change….

For several weeks, a man had been coming to the library every day and just sitting. He would take a book from the shelf and then glance through it, pretending to be interested in its contents; sometimes it was noticeable that the book was upside down which seemed like a dead giveaway that he was not actually interested in its contents. All the staff started to take bets on which one of us he fancied.

"I just don't believe he's coming in here to do research." Melanie said.

"Perhaps he's a police officer and one of us is under surveillance." Sam blurted out excitedly.

"No. He's being far too obvious. A few of them would be taking it in turns so as not to draw attention to the operation." I pointed out. (Like I knew!)

"Yes, that's true." Sam sounded vaguely disappointed "I suppose it would mean that you had done or were doing something very bad to warrant such attention, like spying for another country. Come on Lucie, spill the beans, what is it you're up to?"

"There is no need to contact the secret services like MI5 anyway, I didn't go to Cambridge, so that counts me out!" Everyone laughed, but seriously it wasn't that funny. I am interested in the Cambridge spy ring, but not for nefarious reasons, it just mystifies me why privileged people think it is alright to sell this country's secrets to someone else.

Whatever he was doing, he was there every day; every day except Wednesday, which was my day off. As time went on, I began to feel uneasy. Sometimes when I looked over at him, he suddenly looked away. I began to think it was me he was targeting. Was I being paranoid? Maybe he was just lonely. Perhaps I should go over and talk to him, but I didn't like to; I shouldn't encourage him. I thought he was about my age - mid 20s. There was something familiar about him; I felt as if I knew him, but in truth, I really didn't. How could I? I had never met him before, but somehow I thought that we might have met somewhere.

Lucie was growing more and more concerned. This stranger had suddenly appeared but he was never in the library on a Wednesday, which was Lucie's day off. Was that something to be worried about or was it just coincidence?

Chapter Two

Then one day he wasn't there, he never turned up. The next day he wasn't there either or the next. Weeks went by, and he failed to show. I felt disappointed. Strangely enough, I was worried. I felt concerned about him. Perhaps something unfortunate had happened to him. I really ought to get a grip. One minute I am concerned, but the next I think he is a stalker.

"Why are you so concerned Luce?" Melanie inquired. "You don't even know his name or anything about him, except that he was stalking you."

"We don't know he was stalking any of us." I replied sharply. "In fact, we know nothing about him at all."

"Well I'm glad he isn't coming here anymore, he was really starting to freak me out."

It's amazing how quickly, life can change. We all go about our business and nothing changes. Until one day, quite suddenly, a single thing happens that can alter our comfortable existence for ever. It was late on a Monday morning, when my mum came into the library. She wasn't much of a reader, so I was surprised to see her.

"Mum, what a lovely surprise. Don't tell me you've come to get a book out, wonders will never cease!" She was serious. I felt a sudden lurch in my stomach. I knew something had happened, but I never imagined in a million years, what she was about to tell me.

"Can you get some time off Lucie? We need to talk." she seemed rather nervous, as if she had something devastating to impart. At least I knew it was nothing to do with dad since he had died suddenly of a heart attack just before I took my exams. I still passed and I know he would have been proud of me.

Chapter Three

It was easy enough to get someone to cover me. We walked to her car in silence. Once we had reached the car, we got in, and she took a deep breath.

"Lucie, there is something we've wanted to tell you all your life, but we never got round to it. I realise we should have told you, and we had no right to keep secrets from you. But please believe me we thought we had your best interests at heart."

Here it comes...

"What on earth is it mum?" I felt sick to the pit of my stomach, dreading to hear what she was about to say.

"Your dad and I tried for years to have a baby, but nothing was happening. Eventually, we decided to adopt and we were really lucky when a beautiful baby girl came up for adoption. You were that beautiful baby girl Lucie. Not a day goes by when we don't thank your real mum for the gift she gave us." She looked at me for a reaction. I looked back at her, but all I felt was numbness. I couldn't find any words, so I said nothing.

"This has been a dreadful shock for you, darling but I'm afraid there's more. You see, you were actually a twin. Your real mum couldn't afford to keep you both, so she kept your brother, and with enormous regret put you up for adoption."

"I've got a twin brother?" My voice sounded strange, as if it belonged to someone else. It was my voice but, it sounded far away.

"Yes. The thing is Lucie, he's been involved in a bad accident, and he's in a coma. Your real mum managed to trace us, and she thought you might like to see him."

"Before he dies? See my only brother before they turn off the life-support system?" I angrily choked out the words.

"There's no suggestion of that Lucie, but wouldn't you like to see him?"

I sat staring out of the car window. My whole life had been a lie. I had a brother and until a few minutes ago, I never even knew of his existence.

What could I possibly say? The woman sitting next to me was the only mother I had ever known and I loved her so much. My birth mother, apparently, hadn't loved me enough to struggle through and keep me with my twin no matter what. How should I react? I felt bitter and so very angry. But I also felt both elated, and perturbed that I had a twin, almost an extension of myself; my twin, my other being. I kept saying to myself, *I've got a twin brother, I've got a twin brother.*

Suddenly the car started making a strange noise, the sort of noise that you dread hearing as a car driver. Why is it that quite out of the blue with absolutely no warning what so ever, a tyre suddenly deflates?

"Oh typical, I think we've got a flat tyre, just what we need!" mum sounded exasperated.

"Pull in over there and I'll help you change it. Please say you've got a spare that isn't actually flat as well."

"Of course I've got a spare, but I can't actually *promise* it isn't flat. Let's keep positive though." She smiled rather beguilingly, almost as if she was going on a charm offensive just in case the spare tyre was in a bad way.

"I bet no one stops to help" I said in an irritated voice.

"Glass half empty again, then?!"

"Not really, I'm just being realistic, that's all."

We opened the boot and expressed relief that the tyre looked reasonable, and the Jack was there too.

"Okeydokey, let's do this." Despite knowing how difficult it was going to be actually getting the wheel nuts loosened, I was raring to go. I was eager to get to the hospital. Then, it suddenly dawned on me that I didn't even know my brother's name.

"It's Luke."

"Luke and Lucie. That's nice, isn't it? They go together well, at least she didn't call me Mildred or something!" I really wanted to know something, but was reluctant to ask mum such a thing. I was about to ask a really intrusive question, but I had to know the answer however painful that answer might be. "Can I ask would you have adopted both of us given the option?" That was probably an unfair question, but I really needed to know, or did I? Maybe I couldn't bear the brutal truth of a denial. "Sorry, that's not fair of me you don't have to answer that."

"I'm happy to, and the answer is yes, but that wasn't really an option I'm sorry to say. It would have been very hard work, but worth it in the end. My only regret is that dad and I didn't tell you all this earlier, so that you could have had the opportunity to contact Luke in more auspicious circumstances. I am truly sorry, Lucie, really I am."

"Look mum, we all make decisions that seem correct at the time. That's what you and dad did, so please don't beat yourself up about it. I probably would have done the same thing." I hugged her and kissed her on the cheek. But in the depths of my mind I wondered what life as a twin might have been like. There had been some identical twins in my year at school, three different sets actually. Some of them were really nice and others not so much. I wondered what they were all doing now.

Chapter Four

I took the Jack and put it in the jacking point by the nearside rear flat tyre. As I was about to try to undo the wheel nuts, our Knight in Shining Armour pulled over to us and got down from his rather flash bicycle.

"Hello ladies, can I be of assistance?" *Tall, dark, handsome, here. Eat your heart out, Clooney.*

"You are an absolute saviour. Thank you. As you can see, this one is as flat as a pancake." I kicked the offending tyre to highlight its sad demise.

"No problem. I'll have you back on the road in a jiffy. Could you just hang onto my bike while I sort this out for you?"

"Of course, it's the least I can do."

Thankfully, the man being physically stronger than either mum or I, was able to deal reasonably quickly, with the wheel nuts. Not that he found it very easy. "The trouble with these little blighters is that they are put on in the factory with machines, and when you need to unscrew them, you end up with a bloody hernia in the process."

"I certainly hope not."

"Don't worry I'm sure I'll be fine. You might like to check the air in the spare before driving too far, it looks a little soft to me. Have you got far to go?"

"No, just to the hospital to visit someone, but we'd like to get there as soon as possible, obviously."

"You should be all right because it's not that far, but do try to get it checked as soon as you can. There, all done!"

Mum took a fiver out of her purse and offered it to the man. "There you are young man, that's the only note I've got I'm afraid."

"Well you can just put it away my love, I don't want it, honestly."

"Are you sure? That's so kind of you. We probably would still have been here when it got dark. You certainly are a Good Samaritan. Thank you."

"You're very welcome. Drive safely." He got on his bike and disappeared, leaving two very grateful women admiring his kindness. *Why isn't everyone so thoughtful, he's just restored my faith in human nature.*

Chapter Five

We were soon on our way having waved our kind rescuer off. I was suddenly very nervous. What if Luke didn't like me? What if I didn't like him? After all, we were both young adults and had grown up, never knowing of each other's existence. As we hadn't grown up as twins usually do, would that mean that our familial bond would not exist? I had a weird feeling that despite not knowing of one another's existence we would still be able to sense one another. "Here we are then." Mum's voice jolted me back to the moment.

"I was miles away. I've got butterflies in my stomach. Let's go and see Luke then."

It seemed as if we walked for miles down stark, brightly lit corridors, passing medical staff, patients, visitors like us and "suits" which we assumed were management.

"There's a sign for ITU on the left. Nearly there."

Not long to go now…

A middle-aged couple walked towards us, the woman in floods of tears, the man holding on to her, looking pale and shocked unable to hide their grief.

There was a reception area and we asked to see Luke, explaining that I was his sister. The woman asked us to have a seat, while she went to find someone.

As she opened the door onto the ward we could hear machines bleeping and voices talking in whispers. We sat for a while, a pervasive clinical smell, reaching down into our throats, almost perceptive as a taste.

A young doctor in blue scrubs with a stethoscope draped over his shoulders came over to us looking very serious.

"Hello, we were told to expect you. I understand you were his twin sister?" *he said "were" why did he say that?*

"Yes, I am." I said, determined to make the point, emphasising the word am.

"I'm very sorry to have to tell you, but Luke died about 10 minutes ago. We did everything we could, but his injuries were too severe. Would you like to see him?" I nodded, unable to speak. Mum held my hand, as we walked onto the ward. Four beds containing clearly very sick patients, all unconscious and hooked up to monitors, stood two on each side of the room.

The doctor showed us to Luke's bed, he was still hooked up to his monitor, but it was switched off.

"Why isn't it making a noise?" I instantly regretted asking such a ridiculous question. Luke was dead and the life support was no longer needed. His life had just drained away, how would we know what he would have become? It all seemed so pointless.

His face was very bruised, particularly his eyes, and there were small bloody cut's all over his face, and his hair was matted with blood at the front.

"What on earth happened?" asked mum.

The doctor sighed. "He wasn't wearing a seatbelt when he crashed into a lorry, so he went straight through the windscreen. He had such severe head injuries that it was unlikely he would have survived. I'm very sorry." He patted my arm. "Take all the time you want."

I stood looking at him with tears streaming down my face. It was so unfair, I had only just found out about his existence and now he was dead. I'd never speak to him or laugh with him, or do any of the things that brothers and sisters get to do. I stroked the matted bloody hair and kissed his forehead. As I stood up, I suddenly realised I knew him.

I'd never spoken to him or heard his voice, but I had seen him. Even through the cuts and bruises I recognised him. He was the stranger in the library.

Chapter Six

It was clear to me now, why this young man had been so interested in me. He knew something about us that I didn't. He knew that we were twins. If I had known I would at least have been able to speak to him, but now I never would. Why didn't he try to speak to me? He used to sit looking at books, never actually reading them because he just wanted to be around me; because he knew about us, about our connection. He could have said something, but he never did. Now he never would. I feel lost. The other half of me is dead and I never got to speak to him, or laugh with him.

"Excuse me, I am so very sorry for your loss, but it was my loss too. You see, he was my son and I think you must be my daughter."

A woman stood in front of me and she was my real mother. What could I say? She had given me away and I wasn't sure if I could ever forgive her. Now her only son was dead. My only brother that I had never got to know was dead.

It was the day of Luke's funeral, a day I would never have wished on my worst enemy, but at least in the face of such tragedy, I had been able to meet my mother and maybe we would be able to put the past behind us. I really wanted to know why she couldn't have kept us both, but that would be a very difficult question for me to ask and her to answer, so I think it should be a question left well alone. My adoptive mother and she had become firm friends so I had two mothers now, two special mothers whom I would always be grateful to. I am certain Luke is still around and I know he is grateful too, I can still feel his presence, but for how long I just don't know. At least I had seen him before he died.

Prejudice

Alice was 25 and a dog walker; she had hated being out of work and so she thought it might be advantageous to her and helpful to others if she advertised herself as a dog walker. This she did and was pleasantly surprised when she was contacted by her first client. It was not going to be easy to take on strange dogs, but she knew this was the way to go if she wanted to make enough money to actually live. Having thought at length about things, she decided that she would only take on four clients to start with. She only had a few enquiries at first, but the first person who contacted her was desperate for someone to look after her dog, as she had just been offered a new job which involved a bit of travel and meant that her dog would be on its own all day.

Being taken for a walk by a dog was disconcerting to say the least. Fortunately Neo was not large by some standards; not like a Wolfhound or a German Shepherd for example. He was however, quite strong, being a collie crossed with something quite hairy and he was not particularly well behaved.

Dog training classes would have been the way to go thought Alice as she was dragged by Neo along the lane and out of the town centre. It was a relatively quiet lane, with no traffic to speak of, but as the dog was not hers and was unpredictable, she was not keen to let it off the lead. So she decided to try and make the dog walk properly; easier said than done. After a while though, Neo was beginning to get the hang of it and started to respond to the sound of Alice's commands and the lead being yanked each time he started to pull again.

It was not often that people without dogs came along the lane, so Alice was surprised to see a group of male youths who were crowded outside the large house – the only house – shouting and throwing stones and other missiles at the windows.

"What on earth do you think you're doing?" Alice said sternly, fully expecting the boys to run off. They didn't, but did look a bit shamefaced.

The group spokesman, the more mouthy youth, said "There's a vampire living there. He never goes out in the daylight and my Dad says we don't want his sort living round here."

Alice laughed. "Don't be so ridiculous! Vampires don't exist. Writers like Bram Stoker created Dracula as fictional characters. I suggest you go home and look up vampires on your computer and then you'll discover that they're a myth."

"So why doesn't he go out during the day then?"

"I honestly don't know. Maybe he has some sort of skin condition which means that he can't go out during daylight hours. There are some people who have a genuine intolerance to the ultraviolet rays of the sun. Anyway just leave him alone. If it turns out that he is a vampire though, he'll come looking for you just because you've annoyed him. So I'd leave while you still can!" The boys stood for a moment and then their leader indicated with a nod that it was time for them to go.

Inside the house, the occupant who had been listening and watching, stepped back from the window smiling, more out of relief than anything. He was slightly unnerved when people randomly knocked on his door, and having missiles thrown at the windows was a step too far.

"Would you like to come in and have a cup of tea?" This gentle voice came at her from behind the front door.

Alice thought for a few minutes and then said she would like a cup of tea. The front door opened, seemingly by itself and she walked in and was astounded by how cold it seemed. She looked round what seemed to be the hallway, but as it was so dark she couldn't make out any furniture or indeed anything else.

"Hello" Alice said.

"Hello yourself" the owner of the gentle voice said. "So would you like a cup of tea or coffee or anything else?"

"I only have a drink with someone I've seen first and it would be very remiss of me not to properly introduce myself" said Alice. There was silence. It seemed like forever before the owner of the gentle voice stepped forward to be seen.

"My name is Septimus, how do you do young lady?" A man of indeterminate age with long dark hair appeared in front of her.

"Hello Septimus, my name is Alice and I am very pleased to meet you." She was slightly concerned at the extremely pale complexion that faced her; abnormally pale in fact but his long dark hair didn't really help. She wondered if he was ill, but it seemed rude to mention it and so she didn't.

"Come in please. Would you like tea or coffee or something else?" His voice was hypnotic and she felt totally at ease with him.

"A cup of tea would be great, thank you."

"Do you take sugar?"

"I'm afraid I do." He smiled at her.

"One lump or two?"

"Just one please." Alice had given up taking sugar in both tea and coffee, but had quite recently changed her mind and started taking sugar again, but just one lump and found that both drinks tasted better with a small amount of sugar. Did she feel guilty? Only a little, but she honestly didn't care. She was the appropriate weight for her height and was a little too careful about the amount of food she ate.

"Can I help with making the tea." She asked.

"Certainly not, but you can come and talk to me if you wish."

So she followed him into the kitchen, hardly able to take her eyes off him. He handed her a cup and saucer and his hand brushed hers "My goodness your hand is freezing."

He stared at her and took her face in his hands, "They're both cold and I'm sorry about that."

"Yes they are cold, but there is no sunshine in the house at all, so how can you warm up?"

"I don't like to get too hot and the sunshine is not good for me, so I block it out of the house and I only go outside when the sun goes down." Alice thought about this for a little while and was slightly nervous when she came to a conclusion. Maybe the boys had been right and she was talking to a vampire. It all added up, but she needed to do some research. What did it matter though? He wasn't a threat to her and she really liked him.

"I can see you are thinking about what might be my problem and you have come to your own conclusion haven't you?" Septimus had sussed her out.

"I don't know for sure, obviously, but I think you may be a vampire. If that's true, I want you to know that I'm not scared of you and I will protect you to the best of my ability." Septimus was astounded.

"What makes you think I'm a vampire?"

"I'm not an expert by any means, but there are definitely a few clues. Your dislike of the sun and your very pale complexion are just two hints."

"What else?"

"You appear to be abnormally cold to touch and I'm guessing that's because you have no heartbeat." Alice was convinced that this pointed to vampirism.

"Sadly that's true." He took her hand and pressed it to his chest. There was nothing. They stood there for a few moments, but of course that wasn't actually going to make his heart start beating, no matter how much they or at least she, wanted it.

"I feel like Doctor Frankenstein, waiting to shout "It's alive!" but of course you aren't are you?" Alice felt sad.

"No. I am one of the 'Undead' but still 'living' if that makes any sense." Did it make sense, she wasn't sure but what she did know was that she was in love with him and she had to tell him.

In the darkest moments at night, she had thoughts she would rather not have had. Mostly about what he would do when she died as she inevitably would and how they would both cope when age began to show on her but he never looked any older.

"I think we should be friends and see what develops." Alice knew that one of them should make some sort of decision.

"I agree." Septimus was pleased that at least one of them had come forward with a plan that was in their best interests.

Their lives would be forever entwined for however long they were destined to be together.

Sarah's Choice

Chapter One

There is something wonderful about friendship and being able to spend time with people that you share something with. Mike, Greg, Helen and Sarah were the best of friends and had been taking holidays for several years. Helen was slightly bossy, but sometimes this was quite a good thing as the others needed occasionally to be controlled. Mike and Greg had been friends ever since school and despite not seeing much of each other since they left, they got in touch following university. The girls had been living together in a rented flat and had met Mike and Greg on a night out.

It was really time-consuming, searching through newspapers looking for flats to rent and Sarah was starting to get bored with it.

"I think I may have found a possible flat for us, but it has probably already gone anyway I think I'll ring the number and just see."

Despite being very good looking and very tall – over six feet – Greg was a pleasant young man and could in no way be described as being vain or conceited. Helen was quite convinced that she had mild OCD (obsessive compulsive disorder) and the others did not need much convincing of this, but they tried not to let her get out of control, feeling that if they ignored her odd ways she might settle down. Mike was a dentist and had initially set out to study medicine, but changed his mind at the last minute and went into dentistry instead.

A cottage had been rented for a five day short break. They took it in turns to choose somewhere and Sarah had chosen the area and the cottage this time round. The four friends had been taking these breaks to take part in adventure training, climbing or just to chill out a little.

Helen was bouncing up and down on her right leg; she was agitated but was trying hard not to show it. What was it about people and their ability to annoy her? Perhaps she should just calm down, but why should she? Other people were annoying why was that her fault?

"Come on you lot for goodness sake. Everything's packed in the car so there's no point in hanging around."

"Right oh, let's get this show on the road!"

"Have we got everything; at least has anyone forgotten anything?"

Helen was trying desperately to ensure that a few hours into the trip no one suddenly remembered what they had left behind, as happened a bit too often.

"Trying to keep us in order as usual Helen?" Greg smiled and playfully punched her on the arm. She then reciprocated by using her knuckles to tousle his hair.

"Ouch, that really hurts" Greg rubbed his head "Ouch" he kept on saying, just to make the point.

"Come along children, play nicely." Sarah decided that a mother figure was required so she pretended to sound disapproving. On cue, Greg and Helen, both in childrens voices chimed in "sorry Mum!"

Chapter Two

The drive to the cottage wasn't too arduous, apart from taking a wrong turn which took them a while to notice and thus correct. It was Mike who suspected they were travelling in the opposite direction to where they actually wanted to go. At first no one believed him.

"I promise you we have taken a wrong turn."

"When?"

"About a mile back; we were too busy talking and didn't notice that we should have taken a right turn."

"So in fact it wasn't a wrong turn at all was it? We didn't actually take any turn, we just kept on going." Helen sounded exasperated.

"Are you sure?" Sarah was worried.

"Yes!" The rest shouted in unison.

Greg was driving and did something rather stupid which could have ended disastrously. Before anyone could object, he did a handbrake turn. Fortunately he was a very good driver – he had passed the advanced driving test a few years previously, and never let anyone forget this when a driver was required. Occasionally, however, this backfired on him and he was nominated as 'volunteer' driver if alcohol was to be consumed.

After a while Sarah thought she noticed the odd snowflake.

"That's all we need. Did anyone remember to pack snowshoes?"

"No but I think I packed some tennis rackets!" Mike wasn't one to take things too seriously.

It was very cold and a heavy snowfall in November wasn't totally out of the question.

"I actually just want to get to the cottage and into the warmth. A hot chocolate wouldn't go amiss either."

"Mmm I agree, hot chocolate would be brilliant right now."

Their dreams of warmth and a hot drink came even closer as they drove into the village where they were renting the cottage.

"That's it there. It looks really nice." Sarah sounded pleased and a little relieved that at least this time her choice of venue looked habitable; unlike the one she had chosen the last time it was her turn. "Thank goodness for that. Do you remember the last one?"

"How could we forget?" The others chorused together.

"It wasn't my fault the roof leaked and the power kept going off. At least we got a refund."

"That's true. Let's hope for better things this time."

Chapter Three

They got out of the car and were met by the agent who showed them round and handed over the keys. By this time there was more snow falling and it was beginning to settle.

"Oh pooh!" Sarah was starting to think that a curse was following her around. Her last choice of venue was so memorable in a bad way and now it appeared the weather was conspiring against her.

"I hope we packed enough food. It looks like we could be in for a spot of inclement weather."

"You think? You always were the master of understatement Greg."

"This isn't Scott of the Antarctic and I'm fairly sure things will not get as bad as they did then."

"I do hope not." For a moment they all went quiet and remembered what happened a century ago.

The cottage was warm and had a beautiful open fireplace which unusually was in the centre of the room and so was accessible from both the lounge side and the small - some might say 'cosy'- dining area.

A shed outside the back door had plenty of chopped wood stacked in it; enough they all hoped for a long stay should that be necessary. After lunch they had planned to do a bit of walking around the local area, but the heavily falling snow had scuppered that idea. Fortunately, as a contingency plan, they had all brought a different board game and Mike also had some playing cards with him. Bearing in mind the conditions outside, now seemed like a good idea to start playing one of the games.

"Before we get too engrossed I think we should nominate one of us to be on wood duty. Perhaps we should draw lots."

"I'll volunteer." Mike picked up the basket from beside the fire and headed off "I may be some time." They all laughed at the Scott allusion. The back door opened and wind-blown snow preceded Mike into the kitchen.

Chapter Four

He wasn't certain about the depth of the snowfall and thought they might need more of the wood than he had imagined "Greg could you give me a hand, I think we might need lots of the wood indoors."

"It isn't that bad is it?" He jumped up and as he followed Mike outside he was met by a blizzard and a snowfall of about six or seven inches. Despite the depth of the snow, the two men managed between them to bring enough of the wood into the lounge so that the fire could be kept lit for a decent period of time.

"I've had the local radio on and the entire county is in the same position as us." Helen seemed rather concerned "We could be here for ages." She might have sounded disappointed, but in truth she was slightly excited. Snow fall always did this to her, but after a few days of inconvenience, it was actually quite boring and she was quite pleased to see the snow start to disappear.

"It is a little concerning, but there's nothing we can do about it, so I think we should just accept the situation, get the fire going properly and just relax as best we can."

"Who's sounding bossy now?" Helen said in a disgruntled voice. None of them wanted to fall out, so nothing further was said on the matter.

After several hours sitting, talking and playing some of the board games, Helen looked towards the back of the house.

"Can anyone else hear that noise?"

"What noise?" Sarah listened hard, but the silence was overwhelming. No noises, just silence.

"There it is again."

"Yep. I heard it too." Greg jumped up and strode over to the back door. When he opened it a small dog ran inside. It was covered in snow and jumped around shaking itself and greeting them all like long lost friends.

"Ahh, poor little thing it must be freezing. I Knew I heard something."

"I wonder if it's hungry."

"Of course it's hungry, it's a dog!" Greg rolled his eyes and went to get a biscuit.

"Put some water down for it as well."

"Yes ma'am!" he jumped to attention and saluted.

"You're hilarious, any minute now I 'm sure to start laughing."

The snow was falling uncontrollably and now there was a stray dog in the house, it surely could not get more surreal.

Chapter Five

Helen began to worry about food and whether they would have enough if the inclement weather lasted for long.

"We may need to ration everything".

"We have enough to last at least a week, but maybe we ought to not waste anything, just in case." In her rather over-active imagination, she thought of people discovering their emaciated corpses in a few weeks. She decided not to share that particular thought with the others, unaware that Sarah had also had the same disturbing and rather intrusive notion as her.

"For now, let's stop thinking about food, but I could drink a cuppa, so I'll just go and put the kettle on." Helen was being her usual competent self.

"I'll come and give you a hand" said Sarah. The two girls disappeared into the kitchen whilst the guys sat around and argued who was next to throw the dice and make a move on the board.

"I think I'll just go and see how the falling snow is doing." Greg was a bit concerned.

"There won't be anything you can do about it, so why bother?" But Greg went anyway.

It had been several minutes since Greg disappeared to have a look outside, but he still wasn't back.

"I knew he shouldn't have gone, I mean what was the point?" Mike was annoyed "I suppose I'll have to go and rescue him." Truthfully he was feeling a little smug.

Outside, the snow was still falling very fast. One might have said that it was blizzard conditions. Mike loitered on the door step, took a deep breath and then stepped out into the snow.

"Greg, Greg where are you?" His voice sounded odd. Maybe it was the snow which deadened the sound of his voice, but it did sound strange.

It was a long time since Mike had gone to find Greg.

"Where are they for goodness sake?" Sarah was a bit annoyed, but she was actually quite concerned. "I suppose I had better take a look."

"Don't leave me on my own." Helen was a bit scared.

"Don't worry, I'll soon be back." And then she was gone. She never came back either. Helen was alone; she sat there in the dark amongst the overwhelming silence.

I knew none of them would come back, what should I do now? She sat there on her own and wondered what to do next.

Chapter Six

"Right then, let's get going" Mike wanted to get on with the trip. "Where is Helen, she can't be still in bed surely?"

"Helen what are you doing? I thought you wanted to set off early." Sarah shouted up stairs. "HELEN".

"Alright, alright I'm not deaf you know." She sounded slightly snippy.

"Stop shouting, I'm coming, let's get going then." She looked outside and was relieved to see that there was no snow. "Thank goodness for that."

"Thank goodness for what?"

"I had this weird dream that there was a dreadful snow storm, feet of the stuff fell and we were trapped inside and there was this little dog that turned up."

"Did Santa arrive too?" Sarah said a little sarcastically.

"Look, let's just set off, otherwise we will not have time to explore the area." It was quite obvious that Mike was getting a bit fed up with hanging around and just wanted to get going.

"By the time we start, it'll be time to come home for goodness sake."

They all piled into the car and obviously Greg started off driving, but all had said they were prepared to take turns. It was Sarah who started singing first; she started with 'Puff the Magic Dragon', which caused much hilarity. Not everyone knew the words, but this did not deter her and she was keen to teach everyone the song. Suddenly Helen started to cry, because she thought the song was very sad and she felt sorry for the dragon. Then a big debate started about the real meaning of the song; everyone had their own ideas and things began to get a bit heated.

"Watch out!" Mike shouted "mind that dog!" The car screeched to a halt and everyone sat there hardly daring to breath.

"Have we hit it, have we?" Greg jumped out of the car and looked at the front of the vehicle, but there was no body of a dog; then he looked underneath the car "there's nothing here, maybe it ran off. I didn't actually feel a collision, did anyone else?"

Then a woman appeared from the side of the road, with a dog on a lead. "Thank you for avoiding my dog, he means the world to me." Helen was slightly startled, she knew she recognised both the dog and the woman.

"You were both in my dream last night"

"Really, was it a good dream?" the woman seemed genuinely interested.

"Actually there was a heavy snowfall, and your dog turned up on the door step covered in the stuff, but he was alright and very friendly. We gave him a biscuit."

"Did you hear that Pip, you were given a biscuit!"

Helen was delighted that her dream had some basis in reality. Maybe she wasn't completely mad after all. "Right oh, let's get going" Greg was so keen and he knew perfectly well that any further delay or disruption would result in the holiday being abandoned.

Chapter Seven

The road they were on was very winding and appeared to go on forever. Greg seemed alright to keep driving. Everything happened in a split second. Another car was approaching them when it had a blowout which caused it to swerve onto their side of the road.

"Lookout" shouted Greg. The car flipped onto the roof and collided with the car that had experienced the blowout. Then there was silence. The only sound was coming from one of the wheels which was spinning in mid - air.

Suddenly there were blue lights and sirens. It took a while to release all the passengers.

"This one is still alive so she needs to be transported pronto, her vitals aren't that good. Unfortunately, all the others are dead it was a hell of a collision."

In hospital, Helen was lying in bed, bruised and battered. Both her eyes were a vivid shade of purple and there were cuts all over her face. She still wasn't aware that she was the only survivor.

It became clear that something was not right, when one of the doctors came to see her and he was accompanied by the Chaplain.

"I'm very sorry to have to tell you that you were the only survivor of the crash Helen. I'm afraid all the others who were with you on that day were killed."

It was as if everything had slowed down and was happening in slow motion; all she could hear was the word "killed". Her friends were dead and she would never see them again. All she would have was memories; all she would ever have would be memories.

If she had died, who would remember her?

Lightning Source UK Ltd.
Milton Keynes UK
UKHW021056221221
396076UK00009B/690